For the J's; Jamie, Jemima and Jo (Mum)
And of course, Prue

tukstarling.com

The Blob

of

J

There once was a Blob who lived near to J,

He lived in a cave on top of a fay,

And that is where he did do sing,

He sang the ballads of Victor Fing.

The singing spread to the village of J,

And the villagers heard it day after day.

From sunrise to sunset it entered their ears,

The music so horrid, it brought them to tears.

To stop the noise in the village of J,

They needed a hero to climb up the fay,

But no one would do it, no group pair or one,

No hero appeared, so the crooning went on.

"I will do it," Called Lord Snocket of Snoot,
A world champion climber and a hero to boot,

"I will climb the fay and silence the beast,
And expect to return to a marvellous feast."

Lord Snocket set off for the long climb ahead,

Whilst the villagers went home and safely to bed,

He climbed

    and clambered

        and clawed to the top.

His mission was simple;

The singing must stop!

Lord Snocket snuck into the monster's lair,
Whilst waiting for the beast he straightened his hair.
The Blob finished singing at the last light of day,
Then returned to his cave to hit the hay, on the fay.

Our hero tied up and muffled the beast as he slept,
The Blob did not struggle but silently wept.

Lord Snocket felt proud as he began his descent,

Reciting poems of his victories
and greatness as he went.

As he entered the village with
his nose held high,
Lord Snocket was shocked;
there was no sun in the sky,
He doubled checked his watch
and proceeded to say,
"There's no sun and no feast,
It's the middle of the day!".

Lord Snocket's watch was very precise,
Yet no creatures were stirring, not even small mice,
The village was still and the river stopped flowing,
Snocket left in a grump,
for the feast that was owing.

The village of J was in a deep sleep,

The people, the trees and the birds did not peep.

Day after day the sun did not rise,

When suddenly, little Jack woke up with surprise.

Jack got out of bed and gave his parents a shake,

He shouted and screamed but they just would not wake.

He looked out the window and saw the moon in the sky,

Why the moon not the sun? Jack had to find why!

Now Jack was clever
and it didn't take long,
He thought quick and hard
and saw what was wrong,
The reason J was in a dark pit,
Was 'cos no one was singing
in order to wake it.

Jack pulled on his scarf
and pulled up his hood,
And set off for the
fay
as quick as he could.
Now Jack isn't the
strongest and isn't that tall,
But he climbed the fay
carefully so not to fall.

When he got to the top, Jack looked for The Blob,
And found the old singer by the sound of his sob,
The Blob was still muffled and had given up hope,
Jack released the poor chap by cutting the rope.

"Please Mr Blob, I have come from J,
We need you to sing to start a new day."
The Blob simply said, "You hate me down there!
I hear your complaining rise up through the air."

"I had a job, but now I will cease,
You tied me up so I will leave you in peace."

"We were wrong, we are sorry,"
pleaded little lad Jack,
"The village of J needs
your singing back."

The Blob was still grumpy but was charmed by the boy,

The apology alone had brought him some joy.

So he set up, got ready and started his song,

But stopped when Jack covered his ears before long.

"You hate me , I knew it, I don't know why!"
"No, it's not you, give this a try."
Jack got to his feet and grabbed the musical book,
Turned it upside down and The Blob had a look.

The Blob started singing in this upside down way,

And the sun started rising to start a new day.

The villagers woke up with wondrous delight,

The music and sun composing a beautiful sight.

There once was a Blob who lived near to J,

And the villagers praised him day after day,

And as for Jack, well let's just say,

He was praised and celebrated in his own special way!

The End

all nice,
stopped staring
Feast
hat was
awry.

...ited right until the end of the day.

...stopped singing as the sun se...

The blo...

The blo... stopped singing at the last light
then returned to !

The Story... another ...day of songs.

As he ate
Lord Sno...

He double
"...
There's No,

FRESH
PIES

...no creatures were stirring not
even small mice.
The village was still and river stopped flow...
Snoket left in a group for the Feast
that was
awry.

FRESH PIES

SOLD OUT

So Lord Snooke set off for the long climb ahead,
Whilst the villagers went home and safely to bed,
He climbed and he clambered and he clawed to the top,
His mission was simple, the singing must stop!

of Snooke
a hero
to boot,
the beast
marvellous
Feast.

④

The Blob of J

By Tuk Starling

More books from Tuk Starling are coming soon...

Also available from the
Merry Monsters and
Boisterous Beasts
Collection

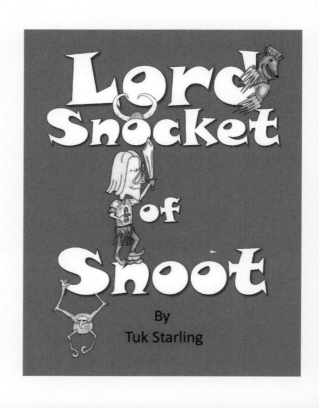

Printed in Great Britain
by Amazon

18687687R00016